THE THREE Little FiSH

FOR MARTHA — K.G.

FOR MY FISHY IVY,
WHO MAKES HER HOUSE OUT OF FABRIC,
FOR MY FISHY RALEIGH,
WHO MAKES HIS HOUSE OUT OF SKATEBOARDS,
AND FOR MY FISHY RUSSELL,
WHO MAKES HIS HOUSE OUT OF MAGIC!
—J.G.

BIG BAD SHARK

ISBN-13: 978-0-439-71962-9
ISBN-10: 0-439-71962-3

30 29 28 27 26 25 24   20

Printed in Malaysia 108
First printing, May 2007

BY **KEN GEIST**

ILLUSTRATED BY **JULIA GORTON**

Cartwheel
·B·O·O·K·S·®

SCHOLASTIC INC.
NEW YORK   TORONTO   LONDON   AUCKLAND   SYDNEY
MEXICO CITY   NEW DELHI   HONG KONG   BUENOS AIRES

Once upon a time, there lived a mama fish and her three little fish, Jim, Tim, and Kim. "It is now time," said the mama, "for each of you to make a home in the deep blue sea." So off they went.

JIM HAD JUST FINISHED BUILDING HIS SEAWEED HOUSE WHEN HE HEARD THE BIG ~~BAD~~ SHARK KNOCKING AT THE DOOR.

"LITTLE FISH, LITTLE FISH, LET ME COME IN."

SO THE BIG BAD SHARK MUNCHED AND HE CRUNCHED AND HE ATE UP EVERY BIT OF THE SEAWEED HOUSE.

YOU CAN HELP ME BUILD A SANDY LITTLE HOUSE."

JIM AND **TIM** HAD JUST STARTED TO **RELAX** IN THE SANDY LITTLE **HOUSE** WHEN THE **BIG** ~~BAD~~ SHARK CAME **KNOCKING** AT THE **DOOR.**

"**LITTLE FISH, LITTLE FISH, LET ME COME IN.**"

TO WHICH THE BRAVE LITTLE FISH REPLIED,

"NOT BY THE SKIN OF MY FINNY FIN FIN!"

"THEN I'LL MUNCH AND I'LL CRUNCH AND I'LL SMASH YOUR HOUSE IN," ROARED THE SHARK.

SO THE BIG BAD SHARK MUNCHED AND HE CRUNCHED UNTIL HE GOT A SANDY MOUTHFUL AND THE HOUSE CRUMBLED.

. . . UNTIL THEY REACHED **THEIR SISTER, KIM.**
KIM WAS SETTING UP HER HOUSE
IN AN **OLD WOODEN SHIP.**

"THE BIG BAD SHARK DESTROYED OUR HOUSES."

"DON'T WORRY. YOU CAN LIVE WITH ME," SAID KIM. AND THEY DID.

TO WHICH THE SMART FISH REPLIED,

"NOT BY THE SKIN OF MY FINNY FIN FIN!"

"THEN I'LL MUNCH AND I'LL CRUNCH AND I'LL SMASH YOUR HOUSE IN," ROARED THE SHARK.

THE BIG BAD SHARK
MUNCHED AND HE
CRUNCHED
BUT HE COULD NOT
SMASH THE HOUSE IN...

THE THREE LITTLE FISH WERE SAFE AT LAST.

AND HE ATE A SALAD.

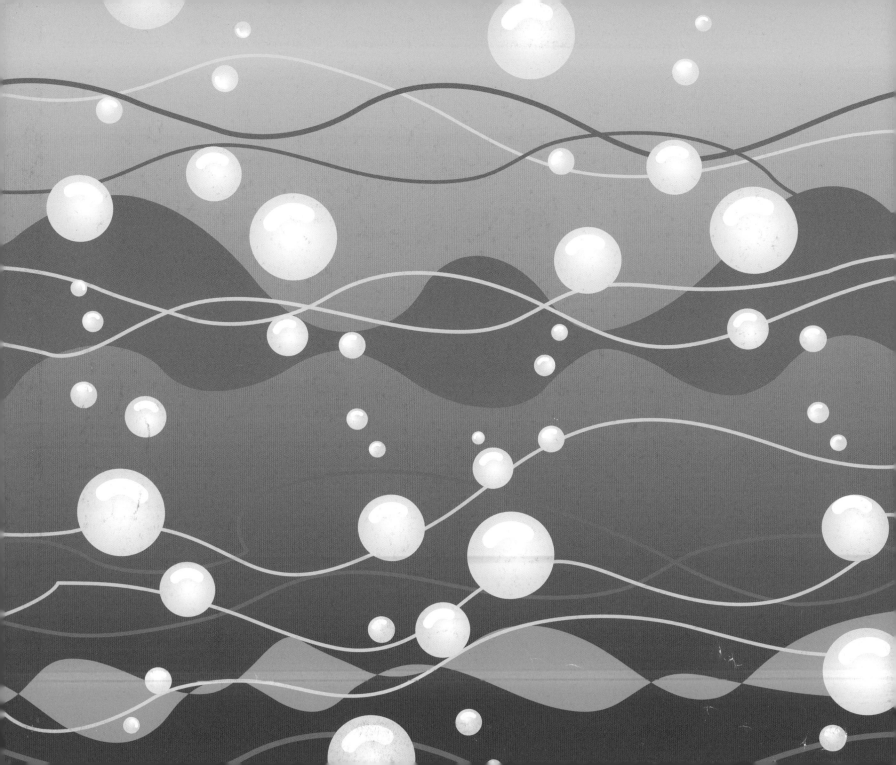